Disney Junior

Fancy NANCY

Nancy and the nice list

Adapted by Krista Tucker
Based on the episode written by Andy Guerdat
Illustrated by the Disney Storybook Art Team

HARPER FESTIVAL

An Imprint of HarperCollinsPublishers

ISBN 978-0-06-284379-1

19 20 21 22 23 SCP 10 9 8 7 6 5 4 3 2 1 ❖ First Edition

Ooh la la! It's Christmastime! It's the fanciest time of the year!
I'm asking Santa to bring me a fuchsia bike.
Fuchsia is fancy for pink and purple mixed together!

"Who wants to go see Santa at the rec center?" Mom asks.

"I do!" shouts my little sister, JoJo.

"Me too!" I say.

As I rush for the front door, I push JoJo aside. *"Excusez-moi!"* I say. That's French for excuse me.

"Nancy, don't push! That's not nice!" JoJo tells me.

"But I can't wait to tell Santa what I want for Christmas!" I say.

Waiting to see Santa, I meet a new friend, Daisy.

"I'm asking Santa for a bike," I tell her. "What are you asking him for?"

"I'll be happy with whatever I get," says Daisy. "I just want to have a nice Christmas."

"*Bonjour*, Santa," I say. "Will you please bring me a bike?"
"Have you been good?" Santa asks.
"I'm practically an expert at being good," I say.

All of a sudden, I remember how I pushed JoJo.
"Well, maybe I wasn't one hundred percent good . . ."
I tell Santa.
"I guess we'll just have to wait and see if you're on
my Nice List then, won't we?" says Santa.

"I have to go do something nice," I tell Daisy. "I need to be on Santa's Nice List!"

When we get home, Mom asks me to collect cans of food from our neighbors.

"Great idea!" I say. "I can do something nice while I'm collecting cans."

I try to be nice by helping my best friend, Bree, fix her reindeer.
Sacrebleu! Oh no! I only make things worse!

I try fancying up my friend Lionel's snowman.
It's a disaster! Which is fancy for really bad!

"I'll never get on Santa's Nice List. I won't get my fuchsia bike!" I tell Mom.

"But you collected canned food to give to the needy," Mom says. "That will make a lot of people happy."

All this time I was doing something nice and I didn't even know it!

Mom takes me back to the rec center. I tell Santa
all about how I collected cans.

"I'm guessing you still want that bike?" Santa asks.

"Absolument!" I say. That's French for absolutely!

Then I see Daisy and her mom in line to get food.
"What's she doing?" I wonder.
"Some people don't have as much as others," Santa tells me.

Daisy's my friend. I want to help her!
"Forget about giving me a bike," I tell Santa.
"All I want is for Daisy to have a nice Christmas!"
"I'm proud of you, Nancy," says Santa. "Being
kind to others is what Christmas is all about."

Christmas morning is more than great. It's spectacular!
Santa brought me so much.
Even the fancy fuchsia bike!

I wonder if Daisy is having a nice Christmas.
"Mom, there's something I want to do," I say.

Mom and I take my new bike to Daisy's house. We leave it on the
front steps, with a note that reads "To Daisy. Merry Christmas!"

Seeing Daisy smile makes me feel overjoyed!
That's fancy for really happy.

"Santa was right," I tell Mom. "Being kind to
others is what Christmas is all about."

Joyeux Noël!

That's French for Merry Christmas!